W9-CEM-159

If You

Believe

A Christmas Story

Also by Jeannine Andersen-Murphy

Fiction

Bloodless

Coming Soon

In a Field of Daisies

The Catty, Catty Ways of Women in the Workplace!

IF YOU BELIEVE

Jeannine Andersen-Murphy

To Beverly -
ANDY -

YOU ARE THE BEST!

HUGS ALWAYS

andy
murphy

BZM

Brzamo
Publishing, LLC
Indianapolis, IN

If You Believe

Copyright@2004

by Jeannine Andersen-Murphy

All rights reserved.

Printed in the United States of America.

No part of this book may be used or reproduced in any manner

whatsoever without written permission except in the case of brief

quotations embodied in critical articles and reviews.

Cover Design by Laura Marie Smith

Book Design by D. Woodrow White

First Edition

The Cataloging-in-Publication Data is

on file with the Library of Congress

ISBN 0-9743580-8-8

BZM

Brzamo
Publishing, LLC
Indianapolis, IN

ABOUT THE AUTHOR...

J. Andersen-Murphy is a motivational speaker and a published author of fiction, *Bloodless*. She is now working on *In A Field of Daisies*, an autobiogrophy. *If You Believe—A Christmas Story* is her first children's story.

Pictured below (clockwise) are her grandchildren, Zachary, Brooke, and Morgan Murphy and her son, Darren, who shared in the inspiration of this warm, family story.

Publisher's Notes

Children all over the world share a common belief in a mythical person created in part by loving parents—the jolly old man in the red hat and suit who drives a sleigh pulled by flying reindeer.

As children come of age and begin to sort through what is true about this magical figure and what isn't, they search for answers. If those answers are not found it can forever leave them with a deep sense of betrayal and confusion.

After all these years, I can still remember the day I had to confront this issue as a child. Like most children who are told that this person wasn't really "real," I didn't punch anybody in the nose or rush home to confront my parents. I simply carried the loss quietly within pretending I knew the truth all along. But, honestly, the holiday season was never quite as bright as before.

This past Christmas, our nine-year-old grandson, Zachary, was faced with his first Christmas without his mother, Penny, who had lost a courageous battle against a very rare cancer. He was also at an age where he had to decide for himself how real the age-old stories of Santa Claus were, as well as searching for his own answer to the mystery of his family's deep personal loss.

A series of conversations with Zachary Conner and his two sisters, Brooke Ashley, age thirteen, and Morgan Ryan, five, about the subject of Santa Claus, as well the subject of losing someone you love, guided my creative process in writing, *If You Believe—A Christmas Story*. It is my hope that when you read this story, you, too, will once again find the spirit and thrill of believing.

In Dedication

We dedicate this book in loving memory of Penny J. Murphy, my daughter-in-law, and the real mother of the characters brought to life in the story, Zachary Conner Murphy, Brooke Ashley Murphy and Morgan Ryan Murphy. While coping with Penny's death, this story came to me and was completed with the help of my three wonderful, brave grandchildren as we faced our first Christmas holiday without her. The answers that we found together carry the real message of this book.

The story behind this holiday custom is dedicated also to my Mother, Myrtle Andersen, who started the wonderful tradition of assembling the nearly 300 pieces that occupy space as a Christmas village beneath our family Christmas tree. She gave us this tradition to keep alive a special place where we could gather as a family year after year and wonder at the richness that lived

within this little village made up of ceramic houses and metal figures complete with fake snow and trees. It is a family tradition that continues to this very day. Mother's little make believe village is a place that holds our past and celebrates our future.

"There are those who live their lives without faith. There are those who doubt what they can't see. The magic and the mystery are real if you believe."

I also wish to thank Jonathan Faber for creating the music and lyrics for the song, *If You Believe.* It speaks to the spirit and celebration of life after death, and gives us comfort while helping us to understand those things that are painful and without reason. I really do believe that when we lose somebody we love, we gain an angel who knows us.

Special thanks to Robin Waldron, senior editor, who guided my words and to Laura Maria Smith, whose wonderful artistic talents brought to life the cover design for this story. I also want to thank Woody White, the talented book designer who captured the warmth of our story.

Of course, I would also like to thank the real Santa Claus who lives within each of us for all the right reasons!

CHAPTER 1

IF YOU BELIEVE

L arge, moist, snowflakes fell silently to the winter gray ground in a flurry of blinding white. A quiet young boy leaned his forehead heavily against the cold windowpane. The warmth of the fire blazing forth from the living room fireplace embraced his drooping shoulders as if trying to comfort the lonely figure. To the observer, Zachary Conner clearly presented a picture of sadness.

"What a rotten Christmas this is going to be," the little boy silently repeated as he moved away from the window. The deep blue color of his eyes had turned almost black, and his fine brown hair was in need of combing.

His smile, usually present from ear-to-ear, was nowhere in sight. Just a few hours earlier, a very good friend, Bennett Brant, had told Zach that there couldn't possibly be any such real person as Santa Claus.

"Zachary, where are you?" the familiar voice called out. It was Zach's father, Darren.

"Hey, son, didn't you hear me calling you? Come on now. We've got to get busy putting up the Christmas tree and the village," he said staring at his son.

The forlorn posture of Zachary suddenly spoke volumes to the concerned father. When Zachary gave no response, his father moved closer to his side, easing his lanky frame down next to his son who was slumped once again on the window seat. Casually, his hand came to rest gently on his only child's shoulder. The touch gave occasion for Zach to engage in eye contact with his father. For a moment, a flash of anger was clearly present in Zachary's innocent and revealing eyes.

"I don't care about Christmas anymore. It's just for little kids who don't know any better, and I don't want to put up any dumb old Christmas village either. It's just stupid metal figures and fake trees and stuff that doesn't mean anything to me now. I don't care if I ever see it again. You can just put it all in the trash as far as I'm concerned," the boy spit out as he stood up pulling away from his father's grasp, racing out of the room where the two had enjoyed so many hours together.

Zachary hoped the tears welling up so quickly in his eyes had not been seen by his father as he climbed the stairs leading up to his room.

"What in the world was that all about?" Darren questioned when his wife, Penny, walked in from the kitchen as the fleeting figure of her son darted past her.

"Do you know what's wrong with Zach?" his father asked.

"I'm not sure, but I think someone told him something about Santa Claus at school today," Penny answered, wiping her wet hands on the blue cotton apron tied around her slender waist.

"Oh, so that's it. Well, I guess he is about the right

age," Darren said, remembering the very day he, too, had heard the bad news about Christmas and Santa Claus.

It had happened outside the Rivoli Theatre on a snowy Saturday afternoon just three days before Christmas.

Darren said, "I was nearly nine years old when my best friend Creighton had done the honors." He shared that it had felt like someone kicked him in the stomach. He wanted to scream out that it was a lie—a great big ugly lie, but instead, he laughed and tried to pretend to his friend that he knew the truth all along. After all, how could anyone really believe in such a person as Santa Claus? The memory was still clear in Darren's mind after all these years.

Running his hand through his short brown hair, Darren said, "Well, maybe I'll leave him alone for awhile. I sort of know how he's feeling." Taking his wife's hand, the couple made their way out to the kitchen where the smell of fresh baked cookies hung in the air.

CHAPTER 2

IF YOU BELIEVE

In Zachary's room the tears had finally stopped, and the long day was now firmly settling in on the disappointed and confused young boy. Laying lengthwise across his bed with his feet just tipping over the edge, Zachary Conner couldn't remember a time when he had felt so terribly tired. Reaching downward, he pulled up the warm quilt that his Nana had made him right before she died last year. There are moments when a person just wants to shut out the rest of the world, and right now, Zachary was having one of those moments. Hiding under Nana's quilt seemed to make it possible.

Closing his eyes, the eight-year-old

boy allowed his body to relax as the warmth and security of his bed permitted his restless mind to slowly dissolve the dark thoughts of the painful day. The dulling cycle of approaching sleep gave way to a quieting, peaceful feeling. The blackness of slumber greeted him with a kind of spinning that took him further and further away from all the disturbing memories of the day. His hurried breathing settled into a steady rhythm signaling the lapse into a deep sleep.

Suddenly, a sharp voice with a heavy Irish accent broke the journey of peaceful slumber.

"Zachary Conner! Wake up if you please."

Struggling to lift his eyelids to the command of the strange voice, Zachary rubbed his eyes, pulling the quilt away from his covered face.

"Come on now, boy, I don't have all day to tarry here." The voice was sharper now.

"Who are you?" Zachary asked, looking at the strange little man dressed in an old fashioned carriage coat with a neatly trimmed red beard.

"You mean you don't recognize me?" the old man replied with just a touch of hurt in his voice.

"You do look like someone I know, but I can't remember from where," Zachary answered trying hard to jar his memory.

"Well then, let me formally reintroduce myself to you, boy. I am Mr. Maple from your Christmas village."

"Mr. Maple? Christmas village?" Zachary Conner was even more confused.

The little boy strained to remember Mr. Maple's face. He recognized it, but he couldn't quite place where it belonged. Could he really be a figure from his Christmas village?

But that was impossible—that was a miniature metal figure, and the village was made up of ceramic houses, plastic trees, and fake snow. It certainly wasn't real, at least, not until now.

"But you can't be! I mean—you can't be—can you?" Zachary's high-pitched voice exclaimed as he again searched the ever-so-familiar face.

"Oh fuddy-duddy! I can be as real as anyone else," Mr. Maple answered tartly. "And, besides, who made it a rule you have to be *real* to be *real* anyway? As far as I'm concerned, there are too many *real* people running around in this world today. Real. Grumpf!" Annoyance crept into Mr. Maple's red face.

"Well, how did you get here? I mean—how did you get real?" Zachary again questioned.

"You ask a powerful amount of questions, lad, and you seem to be intent on repeating yourself. For the last time, Mr. Conner, I'm as real as the next person from the village is, and I've come a long way to get you. As for how I got here? Well, that's a bit harder to answer, Mister-ask-a-lot-of-questions."

Stroking his red whiskers with the back of his hand, Mr. Maple did indeed ponder on how to answer the lad's question. The green in Mr. Maple's eyes twinkled even brighter as he paused to reflect on giving just the right answer.

"Let's just say, Mr. Zachary Conner, someone who

cares a great deal about you sent me here on this blackest of all nights."

Zachary's eyes brightened as the rosy dew of color slowly crept back into his round face.

"Now come on, lad, shake-a-leg. We've got a short journey to take and there are a lot of folks waiting on us," Mr. Maple said as he extended his hand to Zachary.

"You will come with me won't you, Zach?"

"I guess, well—sure. But where are we going?" the boy asked excitedly.

"To the village, of course. Where else do you think I'd be taking you?" Mr. Maple didn't wait for an answer from his young charge.

Placing his hand on Zachary's shoulder, a bright light suddenly filled the room, getting brighter and brighter until the boy felt the whirling motion as the room began spinning. There were many colors swirling overhead as their flight upward seemed to take on an even greater burst of speed.

Just when Zachary felt he was about to cry out the

spinning stopped, and as his eyes began to adjust to the softer light, he heard a second voice off to his right.

"Oh Mr. Maple, I'm so glad you are back. I was beginning to worry after the two of you."

"Now, Mrs. Maple, have I ever failed to return?" said the kindly old man.

Mrs. Maple smiled and quickly walked over to Zachary taking his small hand into her much larger and very warm hand.

"Well now, what a fine looking boy you are." Her Irish accent was just as deep as her husband's.

Her smile was contagious, and Zachary found himself returning it. Looking around the room, he felt as if he had seen it all before. It was odd, but Zachary couldn't help feeling strangely comfortable in this totally strange place.

The room was small but splashed with lots of warm, bright colors. A red tablecloth covered the almost tiny, round kitchen table, and the aroma of freshly baked cookies drifted through the air reminding Zachary of his own kitchen.

"Now then," Mrs. Maple said with authority, "the two of you come and sit down, and I'll get your supper on the table."

"Good idea, Mrs. Maple," Mr. Maple replied as he looked at Zachary and winked.

Seated at the table, Zachary felt a trace of wonderment running through his body. Looking across the room at Mrs. Maple, he couldn't help but compare her to his own grandmother, Nana Connor. Her hair was as white as fresh fallen snow, all drawn to the nape of her neck and wrapped in a thick braided bun. Her eyes were as blue as the sky, and the wrinkles in the corners of her eyes seemed to make them twinkle more. When she smiled, the whole room seemed to brighten.

Mrs. Maple was taller than his Nana, and there was definitely more of her. Zachary also noticed that her blue-striped dress was long, just inches from the floor, and the cover-all apron was the biggest one he had ever seen. It covered almost all of her. His observations were interrupted with the serving of supper.

"Here you go now lad, beef stew just the way you like it heaped with carrots all nice and juicy."

"How'd you know I like beef stew?" Zachary quickly asked as he reached for his silver fork.

"Ah, lad, there's very little about you we don't know," Mrs. Maple replied. Your Nana talks about you all the time, even the little things, like the time you glued your father's shoestrings together."

"You know about that, too?" Zachary's hand stopped in mid-air. His face was bright with amazement. "You know my Nana?"

"Yes, we do," they said in unison.

"I believe we've forgotten something, Mr. Maple," Mrs. Maple said as she reached across the kitchen table taking hold of Zachary's hand.

Quickly, Mr. Maple took hold of Zachary's and his wife's hand. Bowing their heads, Mr. Maple proceeded to say grace over the meal they were about to share.

"We thank you, Lord, for our riches so plentiful, for

your love, which is endless, and for the journeys that have been, and for those yet to come. Amen."

The table fell silent as the three settled into their supper. Three helpings later, Zachary Conner finally set his silverware down to rest. When he looked up, he saw Mr. Maple smiling at him as he prepared to light his wooden pipe.

"Stomach full now, lad?" he asked.

"Sure is. I'm stuffed. Mrs. Maple, you sure are a good cook," the boy added, wiping his mouth with the red napkin.

"Thank you lad," she replied as she began to clear the table.

"How do you know my Nana, Mrs. Maple?"

The sweet old lady's eyes quickly darted toward her husband.

"Your questions will all be answered one at a time, Zachary Conner, but for the moment, that's for me to know and you to find out."

The answer puzzled the young guest, but before he

could respond with another question, Mr. Maple took charge.

"Tell me now, Zachary Conner, are you ready to walk off a bit of your supper? Perhaps we could get a real look at the village."

"The village?" Zachary's eyes were filled with new questions.

"Aye, lad, your village. The village you're about to do away with so quickly, and after all these years no less," Mr. Maple answered.

"I don't understand, Mr. Maple, what village are you talking about?" Zach asked.

"The village that goes beneath your Christmas tree every year. You know, the one that has been part of your family for generations. The one you told your dad earlier that you didn't want to put up this year. That's the one I'm talking about," Mr. Maple replied, his face beginning to redden a bit as it always did when he became upset.

"Now don't go huffing and puffing at the boy, Mr.

Maple. This is all bound to be confusing to him, too," Mrs. Maple cut in while drying her hands on her apron. She motioned for Zachary to come over to the window.

"Here, my lad," she coaxed, "take a look out there and see if you can recognize anything that might look familiar to you."

When Zachary peered through the frosty glass windowpane, he couldn't believe his eyes. It was a life-sized copy of his Christmas village. The one set up on cotton with houses, figures, cars, animals, skating ponds, trees, and all sprinkled with fake snow.

"Oh my gosh!" he exclaimed. "I can't believe it. I'm here! I'm really here!"

The village was Zachary's most favorite thing in all the world. He had always looked forward to setting it up with his father every Christmas season since as far back as he could remember. At least, he had, until just a short while ago.

"Come now, lad, slip into this jacket and let's be off. We have some people to meet who are very anxious to talk to you," stated Mr. Maple motioning toward the door.

"Mr. Maple, be sure to keep an eye out for Billy Joe. Remember what he said," added Mrs. Maple, as the pair of eager explorers made their way out the doorway.

"You must think my mind's as long as a peanut, Mrs. Maple! Of course, I'm gonna watch out for Billy Joe," replied Mr. Maple as he quickly planted a kiss on the tip of his wife's nose. With a look of understanding, a bright knowing smile passed between the two.

CHAPTER 3

IF YOU BELIEVE

The cool air touched Zachary's cheeks as he and Mr. Maple exited the cozy house into the snowy street. Coming from the direction of the church at the end of the street, Zachary could hear singing.

"Pretty good aren't they, lad? That's our little choir. Mrs. Michael leads them in song every Christmas season."

The young boy didn't reply, but simply nodded his head in agreement as their pace picked up.

"You really threw Mrs. Michael into a tizzy with all your talk about not believing in Santa and not wanting to put up

our village," Mr. Maple said directly and to the point.

"But, there isn't such a person as Santa Claus, Mr. Maple," Zachary answered, with the feelings of doubt creeping back into his heart.

"Just like there isn't such a person as me?" Mr. Maple stopped suddenly. "I suppose you are going to say that next." A tinge of red rose in Mr. Maple's cheeks again.

Zachary fell silent. He couldn't find an answer for that right then. Mr. Maple decided to let the subject cool for the moment. His body moved forward, and the walk was once again in motion. As they walked on, Zachary couldn't quite believe the sights around him. There, as big as life, were all the old familiar pieces of his family's Christmas village.

The row of ten, hand-painted ceramic houses that Zachary's great-grandmother Myrtle had carefully made were all lit up ever so brightly just like they always were under the Conner's Christmas tree for the past sixty-years. But this time, Zachary could see real smoke pouring out of each chimney. It was so cool. How could ceramic houses be this big? How could play chimneys really work when they weren't real? But it was real. He could even smell the hickory wood smoke mixed with the crisp air of his new surroundings. Eager to see more, he allowed his eyes to dart as far ahead as he could while he and Mr. Maple crossed the street at Tenth and Nowland Avenues. He recognized the wooden street sign clearly marking the streets. His father had made this toy sign when he was just about Zachary's age. Nana Jean Conner, Darren's mom, always claimed that this was nearly her most favorite item in the whole village. And look, across the way was the smiling snowman with the corncob pipe sticking straight out of its mouth. This was Zachary's mother's contribution to the Conner village. Her sister, Melody Stansberry, had given it to her for a Christmas present, and she had kept it for many years wrapped up in her keepsake box. Every year since their marriage, Penny and Darren Conner had placed the corncob snowman right in this exact spot on the corner of Tenth and Nowland Avenues. It became a family tradition.

Even the cars, piled high with cotton-like snow, were parked in front of all the houses arranged just like they always were year after year. Zachary's father and grandfather had carefully selected the cars from their own personal toy car collection. Only now, they weren't toy cars. They were as real and life-sized as cars could be. It was a bit scary and wonderful at the same time for the young boy caught up in this new and seemingly magic adventure.

"There's Papa's station wagon—and dad's old jeep," Zachary almost shouted as he recognized the cars along the street.

"Oh my gosh! There's my car—the one from my matchbox car collection. I just put it in the village last year, Mr. Maple." Zachary's cheeks were fast turning a deep red.

"I almost didn't give it up—I mean, it was my favorite sports car. Golly, it's so neat in real life," Zachary exclaimed running over to the car, taking in the beauty of something he had enjoyed playing with as a toy.

"So now it's *real* life, Zachary?" Mr. Maple chuckled as he smiled that broad smile of knowing. Zachary wanted to linger a little while longer beside his car, but Mr. Maple gently reminded him that they still had places to go and people to see.

Reluctantly, Zachary agreed to move on. His eyes lingered on his favorite car for just a few more precious moments before he continued on, his hand firmly clasped by his guide's. When they walked a little further, Zachary saw the skating pond where each year his father had placed a little blonde girl in her red skating dress, white mittens, and shining silver ice skates. But right now, that small figure was actually skating toward them, and she wasn't all that little either. As she got closer, it became clear to Zachary that she was definitely the most beautiful girl he had ever seen.

"Why, hello, Zachary," the girl said as she skated to the edge of the pond, stopping sharply, sending a small spray of ice jumping into the air.

"Hi," Zachary responded bashfully, hoping she wouldn't notice the color creeping into his cheeks the way it always did whenever he talked to a pretty girl.

"We weren't sure we were going to get to see you this year," the skating figure added.

Looking at her face, Zachary thought nothing could be as blue as her eyes. Not even his royal blue, little league football jersey that he wore with pride. I'll never see another girl as pretty as this one, the young boy thought. Her hair was the exact shade of the yellow dandelion color found in a fresh new box of Crayola Crayons, and just then the way the light touched her, it bounced a shine into his eyes nearly as bright as the stars above. She had just one dimple nestled deep in her right cheek that made her pretty smile even more special.

"Zachary, this is Ashley Murphy. She could be an Olympic skater if she lived in your world. She's won every contest we've ever had here in the village, as well as in all those department stores where she used to live before your father bought her when he was seven years old making her a part of our family. She's a dream on skates—that's for sure!" Mr. Maple stated with deep pride in his voice.

"Oh, Mr. Maple, you are always so kind," Ashley answered.

"Zachary," Ashley said returning all her attention back to the obviously smitten young boy, "I hope you'll do me a special favor, that is—if you don't think I'm too forward in asking—being that we just met and all. But, your stay with us here is to be so short, I don't really have a whole lot of time to be anything else but forward," she said in a polite whisper.

Zachary Conner felt his knees beginning to wobble. The sound of her voice was so soft.

"Well, sure. Ask me anything you want—anything," he answered.

"Would you try again to believe in all of us here in your Christmas village? I know it's hard, especially after what your friend Bennett told you. But Zachary, it means so much to all of us. You see, we believe in you, and we need you to believe in us," she replied sincerely.

Before Zachary could say anything, the girl bent down and placed a kiss on his forehead. As quickly as she had appeared, she disappeared, skating across the pond in a graceful motion that he knew he would never forget.

"Come on, lad, we don't want to keep your Nana waiting any longer than we have to."

"My Nana! What do you mean?" Zachary answered with surprise.

Mr. Maple gently moved forward picking up the same steady pace. He winked at Zachary but did not answer the boy's question. For the longest time, Zachary continued to peer over his shoulder in Ashley's direction. He wasn't really paying attention to the fact that in just a few minutes they had made their way to the corner of the street and were now standing in front of the prettiest house on the whole block. It was indeed Zachary's favorite with a large wooden front door and big inviting windows that were always lit with bright lights. Zachary had always piled the snow just a little bit deeper on this house than he had on the others. He didn't exactly know why he liked this house so much more than the rest, but he just did.

"I think you should do the honors of knocking, Zachary."

"Who lives here?" the boy asked.

Before an answer could be spoken, the big wooden doors opened.

"Oh, Zachary! We've been waiting so long for this."

Zachary's eyes suddenly grew large. "Nana—Nana Jean Conner!"

Zachary sprang into his grandmother's arms. The two hugged until there was no more hug left in either of them. Still holding on to each other the trio moved inside the inviting warm house.

"Oh my how you've grown, my little giggle-bug." Giggle-bug was Nana Conner's favorite nickname for her only grandson.

"Oh, Nana, it's you. It's really you!"

"Yes, darling, it's really me for the moment. I've missed you more than I can ever tell you."

"But how can this be happening, Nana. You're dead—I mean—you died—you're in Heaven!"

"Zachary, hush now. There are some questions that can't be answered right on top of each other, and we don't have enough time right now to spend discussing it. You need only remember that wishes are very powerful things. When a wish was made for you this very afternoon, I knew it was made at the right moment to be granted—and it worked. You're here with us for just a short while, but long enough I hope to change your mind about a few things, darling."

"If the two of you don't mind, maybe I could rate an introduction." The voice belonged to a tall man with snow-white hair. He looked so very much like Zachary's father, and in an instant, Zachary recognized him.

"Oh my gosh! Are you my Dad's father?"

A huge smile embraced the face of Avery Conner. He

was indeed Zachary's grandfather. He had died two years before Zachary was born, but Zach's dad had done such a good job of telling his son about his Papa that it was easy for the boy to recognize him.

In a few swift steps, the two made their way to each other. Zachary quickly extended his hand, obviously not quite sure how to go about all this meeting stuff. For just a moment, Avery Conner was taken aback. Of course, it was a natural movement for his grandson, but he had hoped for a hug equal to that which he had just witnessed Zachary giving to his Nana.

Avery Conner's big hand wrapped itself around Zachary's smaller hand. For one brief moment, Zachary leaned into his grandfather as if wanting to come so much closer, but he quickly pulled back.

"You look just like your dad when he was your age, Zachary. But I think you resemble your Nana's side of the family just a little more than mine. It's all in those eyes," Avery added.

Zachary didn't say anything. His large blue eyes were

glued to his grandfather's face.

Suddenly, Zachary's legs felt shaky and his head felt rather faint. He had loved his grandmother so much that when she got sick and died last year he felt as if his heart had been torn in two. He didn't have quite the same feelings for his Papa, just yet, because they had never met. Death was something too hard to explain. Zachary remembered with his Nana Jean, he had been sitting in her lap one night reading a story, and the next morning, his father had told him that his Nana had gone away to Heaven.

Death, as it is to any child at an early age, had not made any sense, and Zachary had buried the loss deep inside. Even looking at her picture caused him a certain kind of pain and unspoken loneliness. He didn't have those memories of his Papa. But now, they were both right here with him, and he could feel them and touch them. It was all so strange and wonderful. It was too good to be true. He must be dreaming.

Zachary suddenly moved his hand up to his cheek

and pinched it as hard as he could.

"Ouch!" he said as the realization hit home.

"I'm not dreaming—you both are here with me."

Mr. Maple was quick to respond to the boy's actions.

"That's it lad. Take a few deep breaths. It's bound to be a bit topsy-turvy for you. You're having the same kind of reaction..."

"Mr. Maple! That's not part of the wish. We can't go into too much discussion here. At least, not on this visit," Nana Conner said with just a touch of sternness in her voice.

Zachary's eyes filled with tears as he walked over to where his Nana was standing. Nana Conner quickly put her arms around him.

"Oh Zachary, you've grown so much," she said as she smothered his waiting face with pure Grandma kisses.

For just a moment, Zachary traced his Nana's face with his small fingers. She was real—at least, at this moment. Suddenly, Zachary noticed something different about his Nana.

"Nana! You're standing up straight. I mean—you're not all stooped over. You're taller here."

"That I am. Here, in the time between heaven and earth, that old arthritis is gone. I'm pain free, darling. I got my starch back!" Nana added with a chuckle remembering how she used to explain to her grandson that she was all bent over because she had lost the starch from her body. Zachary smiled and hugged her again.

"Well, if you two snuggle-bugs don't mind, we do have a rather full schedule, and if we're going to get to all the places we need to before the first star circles the moon, we need to get popping."

"Zachary, Papa is right," Nana said. "We do have a rather full schedule. So, if it's okay with you, let me get my coat and we'll go on together. There are so many people we want you to meet."

"Are there more people from our Christmas village?" he asked, looking first at his Nana and then to his Papa.

"Yes, Zachary," Papa answered.

"We're expected at church, Mrs. Conner," Mr. Maple said slowly, as if he knew that Zachary could spend the rest of his life right here.

CHAPTER 4

IF YOU BELIEVE

N ana quickly put on her heavy winter coat bearing all the scouting patches Zachary's father had earned as a Boy Scout. They were duplicates of the real ones, and nothing pleased Nana Conner more than creating this special coat. Zachary loved this coat, and his face once again lit up when he saw it. Papa Conner smiled as he slipped into his worn navy pea coat. Zachary recognized it immediately from the picture his parents always kept on the mantel.

"Wow! You really do look like your picture, Papa Conner."

Avery Conner felt a hard tug at his

heartstrings for that was the first time he ever had the privilege of being addressed as "Papa Conner." Papa wrinkled up his face as he struggled to hold back his tears.

"Well, I certainly hope it keeps the mice out of your living room, Zachary."

Zachary laughed out loud at his grandfather's words. In just a few moments, the love that he had never had a chance to give to a grandfather surfaced. Avery Conner didn't miss the look and ever so naturally, he scooped up his grandson and held him tight. Zachary's strong arms nearly cut off the blood flow to Papa Conner's neck. But at this moment, nothing had ever felt as good to Avery Conner as the touch of his only grandchild.

As they all stepped outside once again, the cold air greeted them; but this time, it didn't seem to feel so wintry. It was a nice cold—it felt like all those times when the first snow fell and we got all bundled up in warm winter clothes and raced outside to roll up the first snowball of the season. It was that kind of cold.

Heading once again down the familiar street with Zachary holding his Nana and Papa's warm hands, the air of excitement nestled in the boy's stomach.

Nana Conner smiled when she saw her grandson looking back at the skating pond. "I take it you've met Miss Ashley?" she asked.

"Yes I did. Mr. Maple introduced us just before we got to your house." The ease with which he said "your house" caused her to smile.

"The lad seems quite taken with Ashley, Mrs. Conner," Mr. Maple added.

"Yes, I can see that, Mr. Maple." Nana Conner caught the twinkle in her husband's eyes.

"Look, Zach, over there. There's the candy store on the corner and the old movie theatre that Papa originally had made from cardboard," Nana said.

"Wow, look at all the candy in the window," Zachary echoed as they passed.

"Every Christmas Eve, Zachary, Nana, and I go to that very movie theatre to see *The Bishop's Wife*. That's your Nana's favorite Christmas movie you know," Papa added.

"Yeah! Nana and I always watched that movie to-gether. It's cool. I mean, there's an angel and he does good stuff and..."

"So you believe in angels do you, wee one?" Mr. Maple teased.

"Well, no—but—yeah."

"Enough teasing for now, Mr. Maple, Zachary will have to come to believing on his own. You know how that works now don't you?" Avery Conner said.

Suddenly, Zachary let go of his grandparent's hands and darted toward the snowman that was always placed at the edge of a small pond where all the animals gath-ered.

"It's the snowman—the snowman!" Zachary called out, his attention and that of his grandparent's were com-pletely caught up in the moment. Zachary didn't even hear Mr. Maple's warning for him to watch out for the approaching figure coming out of the woods.

"Now, now, Billy Joe," Mr. Maple warned. But it was too late. Zachary felt the blow of the hardest pair of knuckles on his nose that he had ever encountered. Wham! With that, Zachary Conner went end over end into the soft white snow.

"Billy Joe, you shouldn't have done that. This is our grandson," Nana Conner warned as she quickly moved toward a sprawled Zachary.

"Some grandson! Stands you upside down in a box to stay that way for maybe the rest of your life," the dark eyed, curly-headed boy shouted.

Zachary sat up in the snow and cleared his head. His nose felt turned inside out and all puffed up.

"What did you hit me for? I've never done anything to you!" he replied angrily.

"Well now, Zachary, it's not that you've done anything intentionally to Billy Joe, but remember last year when you were putting away the Christmas village?" Papa asked the wide-eyed boy.

"Well yes, sort of," he replied.

"I know you didn't do it on purpose, but it seems you put Billy Joe back in the box, well-ah-er-well..."

"Upside down! Upside down!" the angry boy interrupted, still flushed in his face.

Suddenly, Zachary remembered. He was hurrying to go outside to play with his new sled, and instead of carefully placing Billy Joe in the cardboard carton as his father had taught him, he had recklessly tossed the metal figure in. Upside down it was!

"I'm sorry. I didn't mean to cause you any harm," Zachary immediately responded to the boy who had spent a whole year upside down on his head in a dark box.

The anger in Billy Joe's eyes seemed to vanish, replaced with a broad smile and an extended hand waiting to be shook.

"I'm Billy Joe, and I accept your apology," the pink cheeked boy said. "I'm sorry I hit you, but being on your head for a whole year can really put you out of sorts."

Young Conner indeed recognized the lad now. He was the figure in the village pushing the large snowball.

Turning his eyes to Nana Conner, Billy Joe asked, "Are you going to the church now? They're all waiting for you. Mrs. Michael has them practicing up a storm!" he said, answering his own questions, as he was frequently known to do.

"Yes, Billy Joe, we are going to the church. Will you join us?" Nana asked as she gently rubbed her grandson's bruised nose.

"Naw, but thanks anyway. I promised Ma I would get her some more firewood before nightfall."

Turning to Zachary, Billy Joe said, "Sorry we got off to a bad start. Next year, if you let us have a next year, I hope you'll think twice before you stand somebody on their head for a whole year."

As he turned to leave, Billy Joe glanced back over his shoulder and issued a final, but friendly, "See you, Zachary Conner." He quickly put his attention and strength to work, pushing a large snowball in front of him toward an intended destination known only to Billy Joe.

Mr. Maple apologized once again to Zachary as they

continued on their way.

"Uh, Zachary. Let's keep this encounter with Billy Joe a secret from Mrs. Maple if you don't mind. I mean, she can kick up quite a fuss especially since she gave me strict orders to watch out for Billy Joe. I guess I am getting a bit..."

"Don't worry, Mr. Maple. I won't put you in a hard spot with Mrs. Maple," Zachary said with a slight smile as he gently touched his aching nose. "I guess you could say I deserved what I got." Mr. Maple glanced down at the young boy and remembered another face. They do look alike, he thought as they moved on.

The singing voices grew louder as they approached the familiar red brick church with the snow packed on top of its roof.

"Billy Joe is a good boy, Zachary," Papa Conner said. "He works very hard for all of us here in the village. But he does have an Irish temper when provoked, and I'd say, you did do something to provoke him."

Zachary rubbed his nose again and made a mental

note that never, never, again would he do anything to provoke Billy Joe.

As they reached the steps of the church, Zachary found it to be much larger than he expected. This new church had taken the place of the original cardboard church his great-grandmother had placed in her village for so many years. It was accidentally broken when the Conner's had moved into their new home two years ago. Zachary barely remembered the old church.

When they walked through the double oak doors, all the beautiful singing stopped.

Mrs. Michael, tall and sturdy with golden brown skin that seemed as smooth as silk, came hurrying up the aisle to greet them.

"Oh Mr. Maple, Nana and Papa—you are here at last. This, then, must be Mr. Zachary Conner?" she asked in a deep, rich voice. "We were all afraid you wouldn't come, seeing how upset you were this morning after talking with your friend, Bennett," she added.

"How did you know I was upset this morning?" Zachary

immediately questioned.

"Why, the children and I saw it all. You and Bennett were just leaving your friend Paul's home when you started to talk about Santa and then—oh dear! I'm afraid it's all so complicated and time is so short. You'll just have to take my word for it, Master Zachary. You'll just have to take my word!" Mrs. Michael ended her sentences almost as fast as she began them.

"Now come on up front and meet all the other children. They are anxious to talk to you," she said taking Zachary's hand tightly in hers and pulling him forward at quite a fast pace.

Zachary's eyes quickly tried to take in as many of the strange children's faces as he possibly could. They all looked so familiar.

"Hi Zachary. I'm Jordy," the stocky blonde boy announced.

"And I'm Monica," said a small redheaded, freckled-face little girl, looking up at the much taller guest.

"I'm Mario. And I'm Morgan," chimed in two more

children, who were standing side-by-side.

"Just call me Bryant," said a deep-voiced older boy, who appeared to be closer to Zachary's age.

"Well, I guess there is no need for me to introduce anyone now," replied Mrs. Michael, motioning to the children to be seated.

As Zachary stood facing the group, trying to put names with the faces, he suddenly remembered each and every one of them.

Jordy was the figure on skis that he placed on the back hill every year. Monica and Mario were the snow-ball-throwers he always put at the edge of the skating pond. Morgan was one of the carolers standing at the entrance to the church. And Bryant was the young man driving the horse-drawn carriage with the older couple sitting in the back seat.

Wham! Slapping the side of his head, Zachary finally remembered Mr. and Mrs. Maple. They were the couple in the carriage!

"Yes, yes! I remember all of you!" Zachary exclaimed

excitedly with a broad smile on his face.

"Tell us you'll believe again, Zachary," said Morgan with excitement rising in her voice.

"Morgan," said Jordy, "Don't be a pest. We can't make anybody believe in anything if they don't want too!"

"Believing is what's inside a person. Some have a believing spirit and some just don't," added the freck-led-face Monica.

"Children, please!" commanded Mrs. Michael, trying to interrupt the children who were now all speaking at once.

"Zachary, you'll have to forgive us. Sometimes we just get ahead of ourselves with our own personal wishes and feelings," she added with a look directed toward her crowded group of questioning children.

"I believe in you! I mean—I really do believe. I'm just not sure if I'm dreaming, or what," Zachary responded with uncertainty still in his voice.

"Excuse me, Zachary," said the little blonde boy stand-ing way in the back, who had been very quiet until now.

"Would you do me a favor when you get back home?" a shy, Jimmy Grover asked of a now slightly bewildered looking Zachary Conner.

"Well, sure if I can," Zachary replied.

"Would you be so kind as to thank your mother for our new church? The first one that great, great, Gram Myrtle made for us was nice. I mean—it wasn't bad or anything, but this one is just so much nicer."

"And it's warmer too!" piped in Morgan.

"It's the nicest home we've ever had," added Mario.

"It sure would be a shame if we couldn't live here anymore," said Bryant.

"Well, why couldn't you live here anymore?" questioned Zachary.

"We are all here, Zachary, because somewhere in time, the spirit of believing in your family gave us the nature to be—to be here, in your heart, and part of your family's traditions, year-after-year. Well, you, and your family have brought us all together. You've given us a family to belong to, so to speak, a family to call our own. You've given us a sense of roots. You have made us real by belief instead of the lifeless metal, miniature fixtures that we once were. Most of us were products of toy stores, to be separated from our loved ones at the time of a sale, sent into strange places, never to be loved or cared for the way we are year-after-year, generation-after-generation by your family," replied Mrs. Michael.

"Dear me! I guess I did run on a bit," she added with a faint look of embarrassment creeping into her glowing face.

"Zachary, my lad," interrupted Mr. Maple, "I guess what we all have been trying to say is that we would like to simply borrow more time from your spirit of believing. Your family has carried us in their hearts for so long. I guess we all knew the time might come when the tradition of your Christmas village would come to an end. We especially thought this when you were told about Santa Claus. I mean...when believing would cease to be part of your nature," Mr. Maple's voice cracked, and a mist appeared in his kindly blue eyes.

"Excuse me, Mr. Maple, but I can't believe that any-one from my family would forget our tradition of placing the Conner's Christmas village underneath our family tree," Nana Conner quickly injected.

"Oh Mr. Maple, you are wrong! I do believe in you!" Zachary shouted. "I mean, I think I believe. I mean, you are all here, and I've talked with you and learned your real names. Maybe you won't be able to be with me full-grown when I get back home, but believe me, all of you will always be real to me from now on. I'm sorry I caused you all so much worry and trouble. When Bennett told me about Santa Claus not being..."

"Oh my goodness! Santa!" interrupted Mrs. Michael.

"I truly forgot about his time schedule. He's due here in just a matter of hours, and we haven't even come close to perfecting our carols," she said in an excited high-pitched voice.

"We always have a special concert for Santa and Mrs. Claus. They do so enjoy listening to their favorite songs. 'Jingle Bells' and especially 'Here Comes Santa Claus,'" she added. Zachary's eyes were as big as silver dollars by now. "You mean there really is such a person as Santa Claus?" Zachary asked looking to Mr. Maple for an answer.

"There you go again, son, using the word *real!* Santa Claus is real to all the people who believe in him and what he stands for. It's what's in your heart that's really real, Zachary. I can't give that to you. You have to search and find it for yourself. Some people from your world are able to do this, and others—well? For some, it never happens. There's just a big emptiness in their lives. It's sad, but I can't change it. Nobody can."

Zachary's eyes were glued on Mr. Maple intent on what he was saying. The old man's face was kind as his warm eyes looked deeply into Zachary's. Part of what Mr. Maple said made sense to Zachary, and yet, part of it was still too hard to understand.

"I think I understand, Mr. Maple. I think I do."

"Yes, son. I think you do understand a bit."

CHAPTER 5

IF YOU BELIEVE

Mrs. Michael clapped her hand and the children began hurrying back to their seats. They knew that there was still work to be done if they were to be ready for Santa's visit. Waving to Zachary for one last time, the children said their good-byes in unison. With that, they turned their full attention back to the waving hand of Mrs. Michael.

For one brief moment, Mrs. Michael laid her hand on the top of Zachary's head, and leaning down close to his ear whispered, "This year, Zach, our voices will be especially good. I can feel it right here." She pointed with her hand to her heart. "I am so glad to have met you." With those words, she turned quickly away, feeling the sadness that saying good-bye always brought to her eyes.

Suddenly, and with no warning, the huge bells held high up above the gathered group began to ring. The sound startled Mr. Maple. His eyes quickly reflected a sense of urgency.

"Hurry now, lad, it's time we leave to get you home while we still can," said Mr. Maple, reaching to grasp the young boy's hand.

"But, I don't want to go. I have so many things to ask all of you," Zachary tried to say, but Mr. Maple took him in tow and was moving swiftly to the exit doors of the church with Nana and Papa Conner following close behind. Before they could count to three, Zachary, his grandparents, and Mr. Maple were all walking toward the forest of white snow-laden trees. Huffing and puffing, they finally came to an abrupt stop right in the middle of Nowland Avenue. Papa Conner picked up his grandson and held him close.

"Listen to me, Zach. We've no time for real good-byes now, but I want you to know that these last few hours have been precious moments for your Nana and me. You're a special young man—just like your Dad. I'm so glad I got to see you in person."

Zachary tightened his arms around his Grandfather's neck not wanting to let go. "But Papa, I won't be able to see you or talk with you again if I leave here," Zach said his voice cracking. Papa swallowed hard before saying anything.

"Zach, out of sight, out of mind is not exactly true with us because you see, you can talk to me anytime now and I'll hear you because there's a little part of me that will always live deep inside of you. Tuck that thought away in your back pocket young man," Papa Conner said with a smile and a wink, his words coming quickly.

"Papa's right, Zachary, all you have to do is close your eyes and think of us. It's not so hard to talk to someone if you can see them in your mind," Nana whispered putting her arms around Zachary as Papa gently set him down. Tears filled her eyes. Again, Zachary felt a huge tug tearing at his heart.

"Nana, I don't want to leave you and Grandpa—not now!" he said, his eyes stinging just like they always did when he was trying not to cry. "I've got you back—both of you—I don't want to lose you again!"

"My little giggle-bug, remember when you thought you lost your pocket watch only to find it sitting on your dresser behind your alarm clock?" Nana asked.

"Yes, I remember that because it was never really lost, I just thought it was," Zach answered.

"Right! It wasn't gone, Zach. It was right there with you only just out of your sight for a while. That's how it is now with us. We're just out of your sight for now, but we will always be just a thought away from you. All you have to do is think of us," Nana answered, trying to find just the right words. "Listen, when you get home, re-member Papa and me just as we are right now—with me standing up straight and tall, and Papa as strong as he was when your daddy was just a little boy," Nana said as she looked deep into Zach's eyes.

"But I don't understand why you had to die in the first place," Zach quickly replied as he searched his Nana's face for more answers.

"Zach, for all things in life, there is a beginning and an ending," Nana said. "Some will have more time on earth than others. I can't explain that just yet, but I can tell you that when you lose someone close to you, you gain an angel who knows you. Papa and I are your angels, Zachary. We'll always be with you in spirit. Even though you may not see us, your heart will know we're there because that's where we stay now—in your heart."

"But I'll miss you both so much," Zach answered, wiping away the tears that had now begun to roll slowly down his red cheeks.

"Zach, one day, when the time is right, we'll all be together again," Papa added as he gently gave one last big hug to his grandson. "Yes, Zach," Nana said, her voice cracking just a bit. "And as for Santa, and all this talk of believing or not believing, well, there does come a time when a person gets to choose what they believe in. Right?"

"Yeah—right!" Zach answered. The force of his answer brought a smile to Nana's face. She went on. "The truth is —many years ago a gentle man by the name of Nicholas started the wonderful tradition of gift giving at Christmas time. He was copying the Wise Men who brought gifts to Jesus on the night of his birth. Nicholas couldn't be everywhere, so he asked parents to join with him by spreading the tradition to their own families. He wore a special red coat and hat and seeing how jolly he looked, parents copied him in dressing up on this special occasion. When he died, parents were sad for he had started something that brought the spirit of giving to life. Today, we remember him as St. Nicholas. He's the source for Santa Claus and his spirit is real to all of us who choose to keep the tradition of giving alive for all the right reasons. It's complicated, I know, but Zachary, it doesn't matter who's wearing the red hat and coat because the spirit of Santa Claus is celebrated all over the world in so many rich traditions, and if he stands for anything, it's that of love and remembrance. It is a wonderful gift that never grows old, even when you get to be my age," Nana said with her warm gentle smile. "So the way I look at it, Zachary, is that this gift of wonderment and tradition is real. Don't ever forget this or let anyone take it away from you," Nana Conner added, giving Zach one last lingering kiss on the top of his head as she always did when saying good night.

"When you are back home, Mr. Conner, promise me that you will keep alive the tradition of our little Christmas village that has been shared by our family for so many years. Take care of those things that bring your imagination to life—build on them—cherish them. Promise me?" Nana asked.

"Oh, Nana—Papa, I promise. I get it about Santa Claus now. St. Nicholas gave the children gifts to remind us what the real meaning of Christmas stands for—it's not about who Santa Claus is suppose to be, or that we need to get a lot of presents, but instead that we think about Jesus and how the Wise Men gave him gifts on his birthday, so now people all over the world do this as a way to celebrate this special day. In a way, the Wise Men created the first real Santa Claus tradition. So Santa Claus is alive in their spirit and everyone else's spirit who believes! That's so cool."

"Look here, lad," Mr. Maple inserted. "What all this boils down to is belief. What's important is that you believe in yourself as we believe in you. Looking up cautiously at the black sky that now seemed to be turning a bright red, he quickly added, "A Christmas wish was indeed granted for you today, and wishes do come true if you believe. I'm sorry there isn't more time, but the first star has almost passed through the sphere, and we must get you home before it gets past the line in your time zone. Good-bye for now, Zachary Conner. Good-bye."

No sooner were the words out of Mr. Maple's mouth than the whole world started to spin. Faster and faster, floating higher and still higher went Zachary. In what seemed like just a few minutes, he suddenly felt his weight coming to rest on a solid foundation. Hearing a tap at his bedroom door, he opened his eyes slowly, not knowing what to expect.

"Hi there," Zachary heard his father's familiar voice. Rubbing his eyes, he realized he was now home in his very own familiar bedroom.

"I thought I'd come up to see if you had changed your mind about eating some supper," his Dad said looking into Zachary's eyes that were still trying to focus. "You've been asleep for two hours."

Zachary sat straight up in his bed. "Oh, Dad. You won't believe me I know, 'cause I can't prove it's real, but Mr. Maple came and got me and..."

"Wait a minute, son. Who came and got you? What are you talking about? Was this a dream?" questioned the father trying to slow down his young son.

"No, Dad. It wasn't a dream. They were real—alive. I talked to them all, and Billy Joe even punched me," Zachary said tenderly touching his nose.

"I see, son," Darren answered his eyes softening. A warm smile suddenly appeared across the father's face.

"I went to the village, Dad. You see, I got all mixed up about things, and they had to show me the difference. I mean, I know you don't believe me—you think I'm making it up or just dreaming. But I was there. And there was— is such a person as Santa—and I got to see Nana again. And, oh boy! I met Papa Conner, and he looks just like he does in our picture that sits on the mantel." The boy's words were coming faster than he could spit them out.

For a moment the room was quiet as the father and son sat looking at each other. The young boy's eyes searched his father's face for some acknowledgment of belief.

"You're wrong, Zachary. I believe you. Truly I do," the father replied as he reached out to give Zachary a warm and reassuring hug.

"Now, let's go downstairs and grab a bite to eat. Then we can all get started on the tree and the Christmas village?"

"Okay, Dad," Zachary answered. He tried to search his father's face one last time for some sign of real belief, but his father had stood up and was looking away from his young son as he headed toward the bedroom door.

Zachary slipped off his bed and followed his father who was now in the hallway by the top of the stairs. He reached up and absentmindedly touched the bridge of his nose.

"Ouch!" he heard himself say out loud. His nose was still tender from Billy Joe's well-placed punch. "It doesn't matter if anyone else believes me or not," Zachary thought. "I believe, and I always will." A silent promise was made at that moment, which would never ever be broken by Zachary Conner.

Darren paused at the first step on the landing to wait for his son. When Zachary was just a few inches away, his father signaled for him to stop.

"Zachary, can I ask you a question that will stay between you and me? I mean, well, I have never been able to ask anyone this question before now," his father hesitated as if trying to find just the right words.

"Sure, Dad," Zachary answered quickly with his eyes brightening at the thought of a secret between himself and his father.

"Well, um. . ." Darren stumbled over his words at first, seemingly at a loss on how to ask the question.

For just a moment, when their eyes met, Zachary and Darren Conner knew something very special was about to happen between them. It would be a moment held now and forever between this father and son.

"Zachary, don't you think that next to your mother, of course, Ashley is just about the most beautiful girl you've ever seen?"

"Dad!" Zachary squealed out in total surprise. "It was you—you made the Christmas wish—you've been to the Christmas village too!"

Slowly a smile began to spread across the young boy's face, and reaching for his Father's hand and looking straight into his Dad's eyes he answered "Yes, Dad. Ashley is really cool. She sure is!"

Christmas was most special that year in the Conner household. Tradition had been carried on and the reason for believing was given a new, unforgettable meaning. Zachary never again gave a second thought to anyone else's definition of real. That question had been answered for him.

And, oh yes, never again would any of the figures from the Christmas village ever be put away upside down, especially Billy Joe!

The End.

If You Believe...

Lyrics and music written by: Jonathan Faber
Dedicated to our mother, Penny J. Murphy
By Zachary, Brooke, and Morgan Murphy

Close your eyes and think of me and
I'll be by your side.
It's not so hard to see someone
if you can see them in your mind.

Even though I've left this world,
I'm not too far away.
There's a place I've gone to now,
but I still see you everyday.

There are those who live their lives without faith.
There are those who doubt what they can't see.
The magic and the mystery are real if you believe.

CHORUS:
When you lose somebody you love,
You gain an angel who knows you.
When you know what lies beyond
You're never really alone.

Did you ever lose something
And find it later on?
At that time you realized
It was never really gone.

Some things are painful
And hard to understand
Keep in stride—be strong and know
We're walking hand-in-hand.

There are those who live their lives without faith.
There are those who doubt what they can't see.
The promise of eternity is real if you believe.

CHORUS:
When you lose somebody you love,
You gain an angel who knows you.
When you know what lies beyond
You're never really alone.

REFRAIN:
Be still my dear
Nothing to fear
Oh, I'm right here.

Out of sight and out of mind is
Not exactly true.
There's a little part of me
That lives inside of you.

There are those who live their lives without faith.
There are those who doubt what they can't see.
The magic and the mystery are real if you believe.

CHORUS:

When you lose somebody you love,
You gain an angel who knows you.
When you know what lies beyond
You're never really alone.

You're never really alone.

"I've often heard that the best songs almost write themselves. Such was the case with *If You Believe*. While creating this song, I sensed that there was something magical, almost otherworldly, moving through the song. At that point, capturing some of that magic, elusive element became my mission, which hopefully I achieved to some degree. I hope you enjoy this song and that it speaks to you in some way. Feel free to visit JonathanFaber.com and send me an email if the spirit so moves you."

– Jonathan Faber

THINKING ABOUT STARTING YOUR OWN FAMILY TRADITION?

The holidays are special times when family and friends come together to celebrate special events that speak of hope and faith. It's a time for sharing and a time for reflection. When writing this book, I became even more aware of how important it is for families to create those things that will be passed from one generation to the next. Family traditions speak to the heart of small moments in life that will be forever remembered and celebrated.

When my Mother started assembling her special village, as she liked to call it, she did not have the fancy and expensive miniature houses and buildings available on the market today. Instead, she gathered cardboard and cut it to look like little houses, which she then painted

brightly, using color paper to cover the windows giving the appearance of lights coming from within. Later on, she became interested in the art of ceramics and re-placed all the older homes with new ceramic houses. She began adding Christmas tree lights within each house and always remarked how wonderful the invention of electricity was now that it had come to her little town.

She saved wooden and metal toy figures available at the Five and Dime stores and placed them appropriately throughout her Christmas wonderland. To give it a real sense of winter, Mom used a white sheet folded in half and wrapped it carefully around the base of the tree in a square to cover up the old metal stand that held the tree in place. Then she would use white cotton found in fab-ric shops to give the appearance of a winter setting. In the beginning, she would take a bar of Ivory soap and shred it so fine that it truly looked like fresh fallen

snow. Today, we can buy our cotton base and snowflakes in most retail stores, but back then, it took real imagination and creativity.

As a child, I remember watching her with awe as she carefully dressed the Christmas tree with fine ornaments and tinsel. When the tree was decorated just right, out would come the boxes that stored our village. Mom had special rules for the village. Each piece was carefully wrapped in newspaper and placed within its own zone in the box.

Mom had a definite order of where to place each house. It was as if she had intimate knowledge of each household. The Andersen's lived next door to the Fiscus family. On the other side of the Fiscus family dwelled the Eggerts and so on. This was a very planned neighborhood complete with its own candy store and movie theater. The church was always placed at the far end of the

street nearest the manger set, which also occupied space beneath our tree. Next, would come the careful place-ment of each little metal character figure that made up the family of the village. The little boy pushing a snow-ball, the ice skater and all the other pieces were gently placed in their exact positions within this neighborhood setting. Mother would use an old mirror to create the skating pond where the lovely figure skater was always placed. A Salvation Army band and carolers were always placed outside the church door. The carriage with a man and his wife, pulled by a beautiful shining black horse was set on the lane leading out of the city as if it were off on a jolly ride into the countryside. There were the green spruce trees dotting the spaces between the houses and small animals roaming throughout the small park. The oldest figure in the village, the colorful Santa Claus in his gray sleigh, pulled by eight tiny reindeer took their

place on the highest hill that was created out of small Kleenex boxes placed just under the cotton.

In all, there were over 300 pieces in this spectacular little town. It took her nearly two hours just to set up the village alone. I would not be allowed to help my Mother with the set up of the village until I was nearly ten years old. It was a very special day for me and only then did I realize how hard a task this was, as the metal figures did not want to stand up easily in the soft cotton. It took a light touch to manage this feat, and one wrong or quick move could send more than one figure falling into the fresh snow.

Mom was very particular and there were certain things I had to do her way—decorating the Christmas tree and the village had to be done a certain way. This, I learned very early. Today, as I set up this very special place, I find myself doing it piece by piece just the way she did it.

The Andersen's still live next door to the Fiscus family and the figure skater still skates on the little mirror that serves as a wonderful neighborhood pond.

One of the greatest joys I have had is teaching my own grandchildren the history of this family tradition. Today, they are making their own history, and each year we add something of theirs to our Christmas village. This is how traditions are created and preserved from generation to generation.

I encourage all of you to consider creating your own family tradition—it doesn't have to be a village under a Christmas tree. It could be something as simple as making a Christmas apron to wear only while you cook that special holiday dinner; saving the holiday cards that come through the mail and opening them together as a family one evening before Christmas; or taking turns reading the messages aloud each night on the day they were

received. Maybe it could be something else like choosing a special day and loading up the whole car, playing holiday music while driving through the neighborhoods, or downtown to take in the special decorations of the season.

Traditions are important. Life has become so hectic that the time we should be enjoying as special becomes all tangled up with non-stop activities. Traditions don't have to be expensive. Ours started with pieces of cardboard and small metal figures found in a Five and Dime store.

Whatever you decide, I wish you all the joy of creating a history that will carry your own family from their past into their future.

Times past should be times remembered. Sharing that history with those whom you love will bring you lasting moments of recollection.

Jeannine Andersen-Murphy